MOLASSES FLOOD

story and pictures by

Blair Lent

HOUGHTON MIFFLIN COMPANY   BOSTON   1992

For the Lidskies

Library of Congress Cataloging-in-Publication Data

Lent, Blair.
  Molasses flood / story and pictures by Blair Lent.
    p. cm.
  Summary: One warm January day a molasses tank in front of
Charley's house explodes and the molasses carries his house from the
Boston waterfront through the town.
  ISBN 0-395-45314-3
  [1. Molasses—Fiction.   2. Boston (Mass.)—Fiction.]   I. Title.
PZ7.L5415Mo 1992   92-1125
[E]—dc20   CIP
               AC

Printed in the United States of America

HOR 10 9 8 7 6 5 4 3 2 1

Charley Owen Muldoon was busy. Busy watching the Boston waterfront. Busy watching ships being unloaded and warehouses being filled.

Charley's house was right behind an old tank that stored molasses.

Charley loved molasses . . . on bread, on crackers, or just spooned out of a jar.

His father had been thinking that the old rusty tank had been filled too full. He said, "Boston has strange weather. In the middle of a cold January you can suddenly have a day as warm as a day in May. And if that ever does happen the molasses might get too warm and expand. That tank might even explode."

But Charley's father never really thought it would happen.

And one warm January day the old tank *did* expand, then crack . . .

and explode.

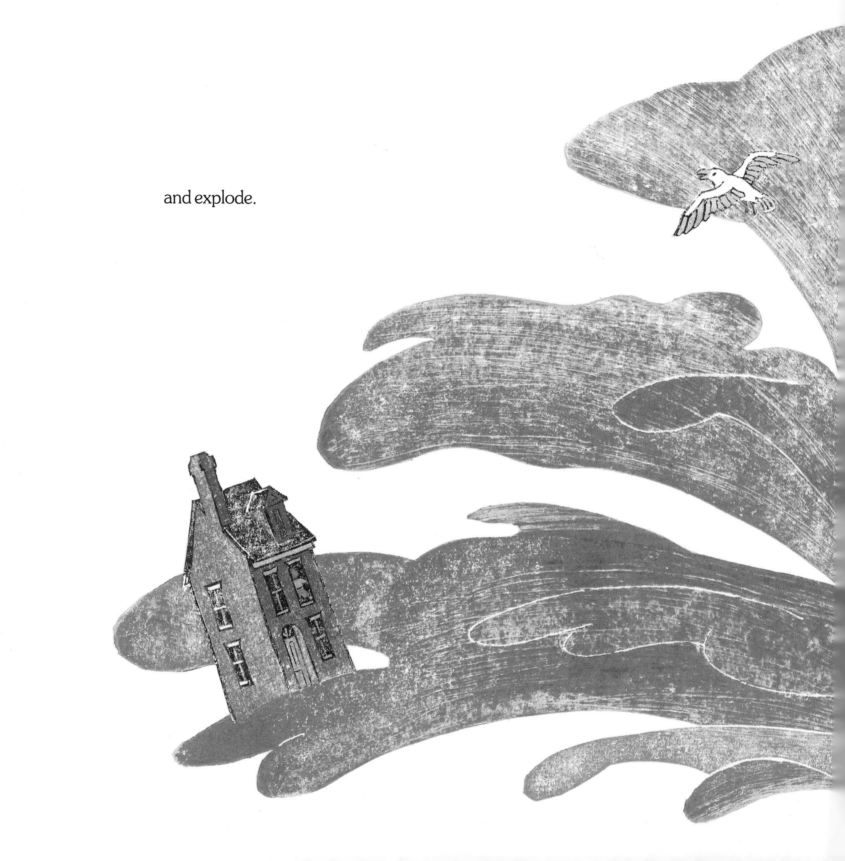

Charley Owen Muldoon ran up to the attic, climbed onto his roof,
and rode his house like a boat on a heavy, sticky, slow-moving sea.

"The molasses is coming! The molasses is coming!" Charley yelled, so loudly that everyone could hear him, long before the molasses reached their doors.

The molasses oozed through the market . . .

and flowed all the way up to the State House, where the governor ran out to look at the mess.

The governor was standing at the edge of the molasses when the sun went down. And he didn't know what to do.

The governor went back into the State House.

During the night it rained. The rain mixed with the molasses. And then the weather turned so cold that the rain changed to snow.

In the morning, the molasses was frozen in place. So Charley and his mother and his father gathered as much molasses as their kitchen shelves and pantry would hold.

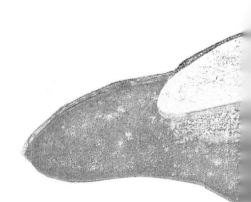

People from all around came into the city for molasses. Molasses was taken away until all that was left was the smell of it, and that smell still hasn't gone away.

Boston streets are fairly confusing to begin with, so it didn't matter that some of the buildings were never moved back to where they had been before.

Charley's house stayed where it was. Charley's mother liked it better because she hadn't liked the damp sea air by the waterfront. Charley liked the view.

But when meal after meal became baked beans cooked with molasses, molasses gingersnaps and gingerbread, molasses taffy, molasses cringles and cookies, Charley Owen Muldoon grew tired of molasses. He didn't care if he ever saw any again.

About the Story

Legends often begin with real events . . .

Once, a long time ago, a molasses tank did explode and molasses did flood a small part of the Boston waterfront. *Molasses Flood* is told, however, not as it really happened, but as Blair Lent imagined it whenever his mother, who grew up in Boston, would tell him about it.

In the book, the Boston portrayed is the Boston of Blair Lent's imagination. The city appears more as it might have when his mother was a little girl. It is a small, red-brick city that Blair imagined in his childhood—similar to a place that is still found in old engravings and early photographs.

Once there was a house very much like Charley's house near the State House. But it was torn down to make room for new additions to the State House. There was also a house, similar to Charley's, near the original site of the molasses tank.

F
LEN   Lent, Blair

        Molasses flood